STERLING CHILDREN'S BOOKS
New York

An Imprint of Sterling Publishing
387 Park Avenue South
New York, NY 10016

ISBN 978-1-4027-9241-0

Distributed in Canada by Sterling Publishing
c/o Canadian Manda Group, 165 Dufferin Street
Toronto, Ontario, Canada M6K 3H6
Distributed in the United Kingdom by GMC Distribution Services
Castle Place, 166 High Street, Lewes, East Sussex, England BN7 1XU
Distributed in Australia by Capricorn Link (Australia) Pty. Ltd.
P.O. Box 704, Windsor, NSW 2756, Australia

For information about custom editions, special sales, and premium
and corporate purchases, please contact Sterling Special Sales at
800-805-5489 or specialsales@sterlingpublishing.com.

Manufactured in Canada
Lot #:
2 4 6 8 10 9 7 5 3 1
09/11

www.sterlingpublishing.com/kids

# ARTHUR
# CHRISTMAS™
## THE MOVIE STORYBOOK

*Adapted by*
**JUSTINE** *and* **RON FONTES**

STERLING CHILDREN'S BOOKS
New York

Like many children, six-year-old Gwen was beginning to have doubts about Santa Claus. Her friend said it was impossible for one man to deliver toys all around the world in one night. But Gwen wrote to Santa anyway, because she wanted to believe—and she wanted a pink Twinkle Bike!

Arthur Claus still believed in Santa, because Santa was his father! Arthur was Mail Agent 3776 at the North Pole. He read Gwen's letter and wanted to make sure she received the bike of her dreams.

Arthur's older brother, Steve, ran Santa's Christmas present delivery operation. Steve used electronic scanners to determine a child's naughty and nice percentages, air jets to erase Santa's footprints from the snow, and, most amazing of all, the super-fast S-1 reindeerless sleigh. Santa's elves were skilled Christmas operatives who made, wrapped, and delivered presents like a highly-trained army.

Arthur's father had been Santa for 70 years. Steve's adoring assistant, Peter, felt certain that his boss would be named the new Santa Claus. Surely it was time for Santa to pass the red suit down to his elder son.

Awkward, gangly Arthur would just have to get used to being a mail agent for the rest of his life. What else could he be? Arthur was afraid of heights, moving fast, and even reindeer!

When Arthur stopped by Mission Control on Christmas Eve, he slipped on the icy steps. Up went Arthur—and down went some elves! Stressed and running out of patience, Steve kindly asked, "Arthur, could you leave Mission Control?"

Since he wasn't allowed to help with the delivery operation, Arthur joined his grandfather. Grandsanta, who used to be Santa a long time ago, was watching the mission on TV with his old pet reindeer, Dasher.

They watched Santa slip on a skateboard and wake up a little boy. Steve used the new Hoho3000 communication devices to expertly talk the delivery team through the crisis.

Grandsanta did not approve of Steve's high-tech approach to Christmas. He grumbled, "In the good old days, you could just whack a waker on the head with a sock full of sand and the nipper wouldn't remember a thing in the morning."

When Santa placed the last present under the tree, everyone in Mission Control went wild. The electronic presents counter clicked down to all zeroes. Another Christmas was complete!

Jubilant cheers greeted Santa Claus as he stepped off the S-1. He waved to the excited elves. Arthur waved, too, though his tired, preoccupied father did not notice.

Santa addressed the happy crowd. "Tonight we delivered two billion presents! My biggest year ever!" He thanked Steve, saying, "I couldn't do it without you!" He also thanked Mrs. Claus, Grandsanta, and almost forgot to mention Arthur. "I can't wait for year seventy-one!" Santa said.

Everyone expected Santa to say that Steve would be taking over his job. The elves mistakenly released a banner and balloons congratulating Steve. Assuming all the fuss was for him, Santa did not even notice.

After the celebration, a hardworking elf named Bryony cleaned the dock. Amid tattered wrappings, she found one lone gift that had fallen off the conveyor belt by accident. Bryony immediately reported this on her Hoho3000.

Steve could not believe it. "The system is foolproof!"

Peter scanned the tag and reported, "47785BXK did NOT get the wrong gift . . . Or . . . um, the right one."

Arthur gasped. "So somebody got . . . nothing? At all?"

Steve told Santa that they could not deliver the present. The S-1 could not safely fly again without maintenance. Instead, he suggested Santa send the gift by express mail. A few days wouldn't matter.

"That'll ruin the magic!" Arthur exclaimed.

"I won't sleep easy after this. But it can't be helped," Santa said.

Arthur and Bryony were stunned. Deciding to take matters into their own not-very-capable hands, Bryony and Arthur matched the gift's tag to Gwen's postcard. Arthur wondered how he could possibly get Gwen's pink Twinkle Bike to England, halfway around the world, before sunrise!

Arthur felt miserable about this impossible situation, but Grandsanta thought it was funny. "So much for yer brother's fancy-pants technology!" Then he showed Arthur something that was supposed to have been scrapped years before, his old wooden sleigh, Eve. "But there is a way, Arthur." In a nearby stable were eight reindeer, the great-great-grandchildren of the original eight.

Grandsanta could deliver Gwen's gift—but he wouldn't do it alone. The old man insisted that Arthur come along.

Arthur protested, "I'm scared of heights, speed, and reindeer! I can't even ride a bike without training wheels."

But he also couldn't bear the thought of any child waking up to no gift from Santa under the tree. So he climbed into the sleigh.

Grandsanta flicked the reins and sprinkled the deer with magic dust, and the sleigh floated off the ground! Arthur screamed!

As the sleigh shot up into the frosty night, Arthur thought he was having a heart attack. Grandsanta whooped with glee.

Grandsanta pulled out an ancient map, the map that had been used by the Clauses every Christmas night in history. He stared at the stars and remarked, "It's the same old world!"

But it wasn't! Since the map was made, an entire city had sprung up, full of skyscrapers, satellite dishes, signs, and cables. Arthur screamed as the sleigh narrowly missed a giant clock. Then Grandsanta discovered a stowaway aboard Eve.

"Bryony Shelfley, Wrapping Operative Grade 3!" the stowaway replied. "I can wrap anything, sir."

"Good. Wrap yourself a parachute," Grandsanta snapped as he tossed the elf overboard.

Arthur gasped in horror, but the resourceful elf quickly taped herself to the sleigh.

With Bryony safely on board, they soon realized the sleigh was hopelessly off course. They landed the sleigh—only to discover on the Hoho3000 GPS that they were in Africa!

Moments later, lions began to circle Grandsanta, Bryony, and Arthur.

Arthur's singing reindeer slippers briefly distracted the hungry lions threatening to eat the three travelers. Then Bryony wrapped the beasts until the sleigh could take to the skies again. During the desperate escape, some magic dust fell on the animals. Soon even the elephants started floating above the savannah!

Steve's recorded GPS voice recited a new route on the Hoho3000. When the sleigh landed, Arthur and Bryony cheered, "We did it!"

"Whoopee doo," Grandsanta sneered. His camera was broken during the lion attack. He would never get a picture of himself saving the day now. That was why he wanted to deliver the present.

Arthur's heart sank as he realized his grandfather only wanted to prove to his dad and Steve that he was the best Santa.

MIMOSA AV.

Despite their disappointment with Grandsanta, Arthur and Bryony snuck into the house at 23 Mimosa Avenue. Unfortunately, there was already a gift from Santa under the tree.

Meanwhile in Mission Control, Steve was horrified to learn that every nation on earth was tracking Santa's sleigh! Steve moaned, "Two billion items delivered and we didn't leave a footprint in the snow. And now . . . ?"

Bryony realized their mistake. They were in Trelew, MEXICO!
They had to make it to England before sunrise.

Arthur taped himself to the sleigh and declared, "We just have to
go faster . . . higher!"

Then Bryony's Hoho3000 rang and a very angry Steve was on the
other end. Grandsanta tried to blame Arthur for the unauthorized
trip, but Steve saw through him. With no fight left in him,
Grandsanta promised to come home immediately.

"What about Gwen? We can't let her down!" Arthur objected and begged his brother to consult with Santa.

"He went to bed!" Steve exclaimed.

Arthur disagreed. "He's lying awake, worrying his beard off!"

Exasperated, Steve pressed the big red Santa button. The answering machine clicked on, "Ho, ho, ho, getting some shut-eye, please do not disturb me until New Years Day."

Arthur felt so stunned he lost control of the reins. The sleigh flipped upside down and dumped the three of them on a beach in Cuba!

Back at the North Pole, a group of confused elves woke Santa up. "Is it true you missed a child?" they asked, not wanting to believe it.

Santa tried to remember what Steve had said, but that only upset the elves more.

An elf asked, "Sir, if the one that got missed doesn't matter—why have Arthur and Grandsanta gone to deliver the gift?"

Santa and his wife rushed to Mission Control where they found Steve staring at screens full of sleigh sightings. Where was Arthur? Santa searched Arthur's office for clues. When he saw all the touching Christmas knick-knacks, Santa felt very ashamed. Arthur believed in Christmas. Arthur believed in him.

Back in Cuba, Arthur sank deeper into despair. Then, suddenly, he lifted up Gwen's letter. It had a drawing of Santa on it.

"This is Santa!" he exclaimed to Grandsanta. "As long as the bike is there when Gwen wakes up, she will know that Santa came, and he cares."

Arthur borrowed a boat and started frantically rowing. Grandsanta had seen this kind of madness before. "He's suffering from 'sleigh fever,'" he told the elf.

Bryony checked her Hoho3000. "Do you really think you can row the Atlantic in 37 minutes?"

Grandsanta pointed out that they weren't the only ones going in circles. "The reindeer will just keep flying. They'll pass right over us."

That gave Arthur an idea. "Then we CAN get the sleigh back!"

Grandsanta thought Arthur's plan was absolutely bonkers. "You want to catch the sleigh with this anchor?"

All Arthur needed was some magic dust. Luckily, Bryony had some in her Emergency Cracker. This was not going to be easy. The sleigh would be coming toward Arthur at 45,000 miles per hour!

Arthur knew one thing more frightening than floating into space to catch a speeding sleigh: the thought of disappointing a child.

Just as Bryony tied a ribbon around his waist, he pulled the cracker. Shaking, Arthur floated up like a living balloon.

Suddenly, with a high-speed jingle of bells, the sleigh appeared! Arthur swung the anchor and . . . it snagged the reindeer harness. The sleigh towed him away with a rush of wind and sheer velocity!

Powered by panic, Arthur finally scrambled into the sleigh. He tugged the handbrake. The sleigh abruptly dropped down right above Bryony and Grandsanta!

The rapidly descending reindeer broke the boat, but bounced the elf and the old man into the sleigh. Bryony flung her arms around Arthur.

"Yay! Arthur! You did it! I thought for sure you'd die! But you did it!"

Amid the wreckage of the boat, a robotic voice recited, "Proceed to the highlighted rou . . . gurgle, gurgle." Bryony's Hoho3000 sank into the sea.

Grandsanta seized the reins. "To Trelew!" he commanded!

Meanwhile, at the North Pole, Santa and Mrs. Claus prepared to take off, too. Santa was determined to deliver the present and rescue his son and father. Unfortunately, Santa had no idea how to drive the S-1. So the sleigh strained at its cables and rammed into the nearest ice wall, inflating the airbag.

Steve ranted, "You dented it! You took it out without permission and . . ."

Mrs. Claus shouted, "FOR GOODNESS SAKE! Arthur and Grandsanta are out there, and you two are bickering over a big red toy?"

Santa asked his son to drive, and they were off with a *VROOOM!*

When the elves saw the S-1 leaving, they panicked! They thought the Clauses were deserting them. What would they do without Santa Claus?

"It's the end of Christmas!" an elf despaired.

"Abandon the North Pole!" another suggested hysterically.

Amid the chaos, Peter made his way to Steve's control panel. The assistant swore, "I'll stop him for you, sir! The true Santa will rise!"

Far away, the battered old sleigh rose to new heights. But the sun was rapidly rising. Soon the line of daylight would reach England—and they could not let it arrive before they delivered Gwen's bike!

Surrounded by the world's military leaders, Chief DeSilva
watched Arthur's sleigh streaking across a bank of screens. It
looked like a UFO! Then an urgent call came in.

The shrill voice on the speakerphone shouted, "It's not a
sleigh . . . It's aliens! They're heading for England! Tell the British
army to shoot 'em down! I'm the British King . . . I mean the
Prime Minister," Peter fibbed hastily. "I'm not an elf!"

The generals agreed that they had to shoot down the red thing.

Grandsanta's sleigh struggled to hold its course as tremendous speed threatened to tear it to pieces! Then the reindeer broke free. Who would pull their sleigh?

Dasher climbed clumsily over Grandsanta.

"Not now, you sack of antlers!" he complained.

But Dasher wasn't trying to sit in the old man's lap. The ancient reindeer grabbed the harness with his teeth, determined to pull that sleigh!

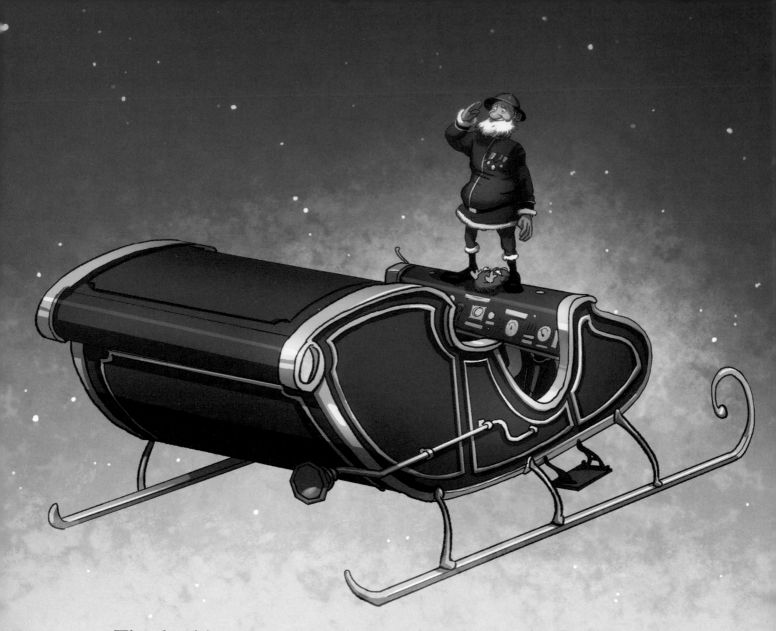

The sleigh's passengers encouraged Dasher by singing, "Jingle Bells." Unfortunately, Arthur's musical slipper joined in, too. The shoe's battery gave the missile an electronic signal to track.

Grandsanta grabbed the slipper. "I'll create a diversion."

In seconds, Arthur and Bryony dropped down through the sky. Their makeshift parachute was actually a giant red velvet sack, the very bag that had once held toys for all the children of the world.

Grandsanta loosened Dasher's reins and declared, "This is it, old fella." With the missile whistling in his ears, the loyal reindeer floated free.

A few seconds later, De Silva received the report: "Red thing down."

Meanwhile at 23 Mimosa Avenue, Steve launched into his speech. "Good morning, Gwen. Ho, ho, etcetera. Apologies for the minor delay. As a goodwill gesture, I've upgraded you to the Glamourfest Ultra X-3 bike."

But the child was a little boy, not Gwen at all! Steve was at the wrong house in the wrong country speaking the wrong language!

Arthur and Bryony were also having problems. They could see Trelew but it was over a mile away.

Arthur's leg ached from their fall, but he didn't care. He hadn't come this far to fail. Arthur pulled just enough paper off Gwen's bike to let down the training wheels and said, "I can cycle." Then he took off.

Bryony ran after him. "Come back! What about the wrapping?!"

The bicycle and the running elf soon sped past a trash bin where Dasher sniffed out Grandsanta. The old man was confused but alive!

Meanwhile, Steve returned to the S-1. He grumbled, "OK, so I'm not great with children! You're hardly perfect. Let me guess, you put in the address, then clicked on the first Mimosa Avenue. You're just like Arthur!"

"Am I?" Santa hoped this was true.

Just then, the Clauses received a message from Mission Control: The sleigh had been shot, but Arthur was still going!

The pink Twinkle Bike rolled toward Mimosa Avenue. Bryony trotted breathlessly behind Arthur, fretting, "You're getting it dirty!" But Arthur refused to slow down. Bryony started wrapping the moving bicycle, "No one gets an unwrapped gift on my watch."

But just then the sun's first ray kissed Gwen's face. Her eyes fluttered open.

Arthur exclaimed in anguish. "No! We can't be too late!"

Suddenly a huge shadow fell over the quiet avenue, turning dawn into night. Gwen drifted back to sleep, her bedroom shaded by the well-timed arrival of the S-1.

As Arthur struggled to climb in a window with the bike, Steve and Santa descended from the S-1. But they weren't the only Santas on the scene . . .

. . . Grandsanta was also determined to make that delivery. Still groggy from the missile, the old man thought the trash bin Dasher pulled was his sleigh and the garbage bag he carried was full of candy and toys!

Arthur was moved by his father's presence. "I knew you wouldn't just go to bed and forget Gwen. You're Santa!"

Before Santa could admit the truth, Steve and Grandsanta grabbed at the bike.

"I'm Santa! I'm delivering it!" Steve asserted.

"I'm Santa. Can't you see from my suit?" the old man demanded.

"I am actually Santa," Santa pointed out.

Upstairs a six-year-old's excited voice exclaimed, "It's Christmas!"

"Please," Arthur begged. "Gwen *must* have a present from Santa!"

His father recognized all that was Santa in Arthur. He certainly had the heart. Santa said, "You do it, Arthur."

So the youngest Claus dashed into the living room to tuck the gift under the tree.

Then, just in time, the Clauses hid in the nearby closet. In his seventy years as Santa, Arthur's father had never witnessed this precious moment. He was always gone before children found their presents.

"Mummy, Daddy, come ON! Look!" Gwen exclaimed at the sight of Bryony's beautifully wrapped bike.

Gwen tore through the bright paper, heart thumping with giddy anticipation. "Oh look! What is it?" The little girl's joy was contagious. This wasn't just any bike. It was the very pink Twinkle Bicycle the little girl had requested in her letter.

All the Clauses shared Gwen's bliss. This was Christmas!

Steve's mind had always been on the slick sleigh, cool suit, and ever-more-efficient deliveries. He'd never pictured such joy over one toy.

Santa said, "Steve, you deserve to be Santa. But . . ." He looked at Arthur.

Steve felt grateful for this acknowledgement of his hard work, but he agreed that Arthur already was Santa.

Arthur could hardly
believe the good news.
He was now Santa Claus!

Looking in the window, Bryony felt proud to share in Arthur's success.
The last, lost gift, perfectly wrapped, had finally been delivered.

All the elves in Mission Control were thrilled. A gift for every child;
another successful season and . . . a new Santa!

Above Mimosa Avenue, Grandsanta, Steve, and Santa were pulled
into the S-1. Unfortunately, Arthur was still something of a klutz. On
his way up to the sleigh, Arthur banged into a tree and fell in the snow.

When he stood up, the wind filled his red parka. For one magical moment, Gwen glimpsed what looked like a jolly, white-bearded fat man in a red suit. Could it really be Santa Claus?

Then the vision was gone. Even though she would never know for sure if she had actually seen him, Gwen would always believe in Santa Claus.

# Behind the Scenes

The amazing art and dynamic animation for *Arthur Christmas* was not made overnight. It took artists years to perfect every last detail of the characters and environments. Before making it to the big screen, the talented teams at Aardman Animations and Sony Pictures Animation created hundreds of character and location sketches, sculptures, and paintings for inspiration. Their CG (computer-generated) experts then took that hand-drawn artwork and used it as a basis for the final film you see in theaters. Here is some "behind-the-scenes" art that shows how *Arthur Christmas* came to life!

*Sketch and final painting of Mrs. Claus*

*Early charcoal drawing of Arthur in his office*

*Painting of Arthur entering Mission Control*

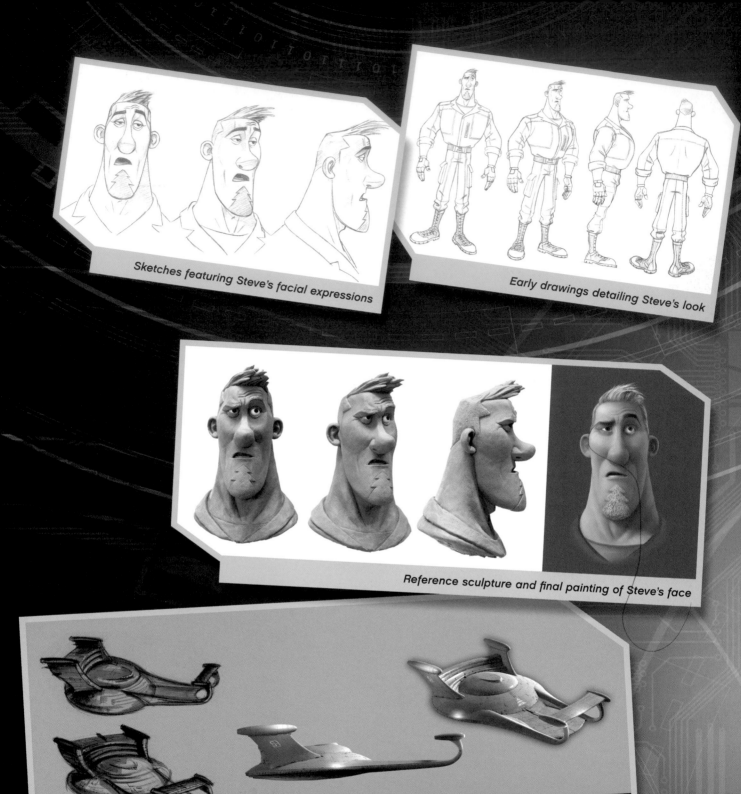

Sketches featuring Steve's facial expressions

Early drawings detailing Steve's look

Reference sculpture and final painting of Steve's face

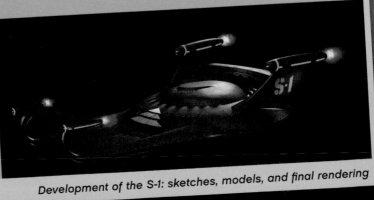

Development of the S-1: sketches, models, and final rendering

Painting of Arthur's exciting journey through Toronto

The planning of Mission Control and a painting of its final design

Sketch of Steve showing off his confidence

47

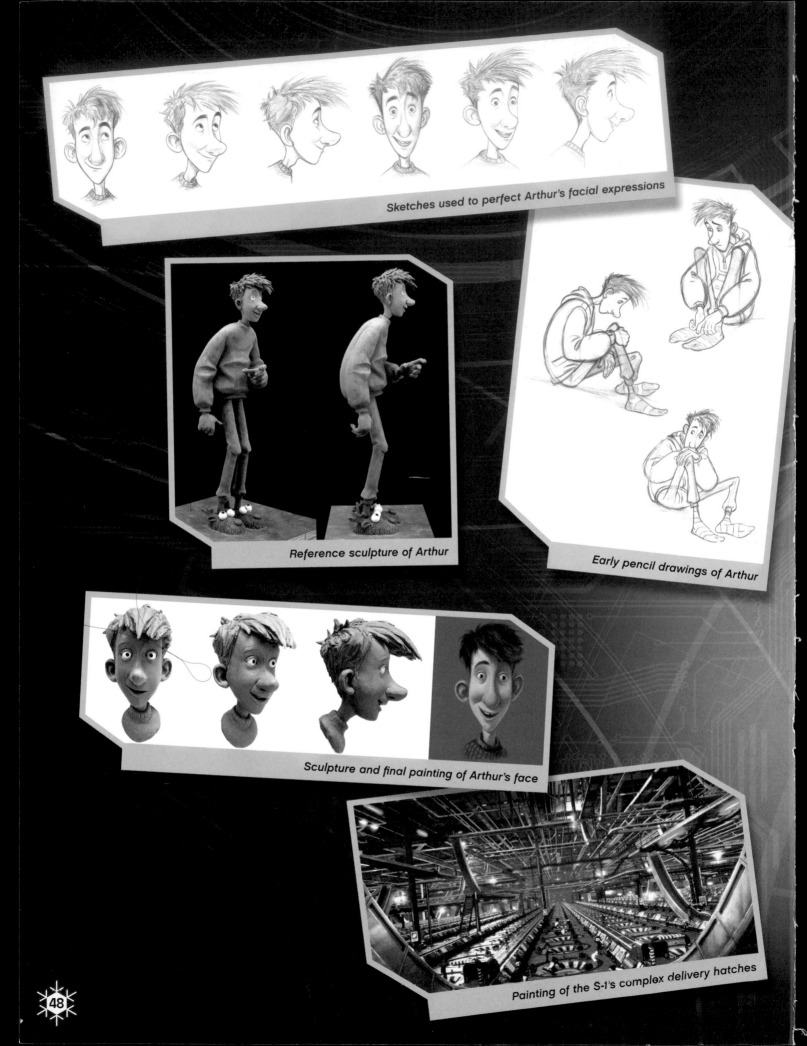

Sketches used to perfect Arthur's facial expressions

Reference sculpture of Arthur

Early pencil drawings of Arthur

Sculpture and final painting of Arthur's face

Painting of the S-1's complex delivery hatches

48